Annie's World

There are rainbows in the sand

For more information and other book titles please visit

www.familyfeelings.today

Contents

CHAPTER ONE

I kick the heap of slimy seaweed and bend down.
A hermit crab scuttles off. Empty seashells shine
blue and silver. I pop them in my pocket, which is
nearly full, and as I run down the beach all the shells
rattle and clink. This is my third favourite sound.
My second favourite is hearing big waves crashing
on the shore. My absolute first favourite sound of

all, though, is the shoofle the sea makes when it sucks the water out across the pebbles and sand.

I call for Echo and he comes scampering across from the rock pool where he's been pawing for imaginary fish. As he reaches me he stops and sticks his wet, black nose into my hand. Echo is my lurcher dog, and he's my very best friend.

We run together across the beach and catch up with Grandad and Tim. Tim is building another castle right by the edge, jumping up and down as the water crumbles it down. For a little brother, he's pretty cute. He's three and I'm ten.

Grandad is looking up at the seagulls high above the sea. I grab his hand, and we both grab Tim and swing him up into the air again and again as we walk back home. Echo wuffs every time Tim squeals, but they're happy noises and they make me feel happy.

If I could, I'd come to the beach every single day. We nearly do, but nearly isn't enough. When I'm by the sea everything that feels cross and sad and scared and mad seems to drift away. I can come down here heavy as wet sand underwater, and leave like the dusty powder by the dunes.

Tim and I live with Mum and Grandad in a house squished between two others with a long back garden. Echo races us up and down and round the bushes every morning when we let him out. I like the way the outside porch light flickers on when we walk up the drive, welcoming us home. When we get back today, Tim starts squeaking for his tea. It's five o'clock. Mum should be home in fifteen minutes.

'Annie, come and help me with the vegetables.'

Grandad likes me to keep him company while he cooks.

I enjoy bits about being in the kitchen, especially investigating the contents of the biscuit tin, but dinnertime makes the room noisy and hot. It's full of different cooking smells and my nose doesn't know what it's sniffing first.

Grandad gives me a vegetable peeler and a bag full of bright-orange carrots. The peeler makes a sharp swipe as I take the skin away. He is slicing onions and splashing them into the frying pan. The chop-chop and sizzling tickles my brain.

When he puts the carrots on to boil, the room fills with steam and my glasses get all foggy. Then the oven buzzer goes off. I have to get out.

'Grandad, I'm going to check on Tim.'

'Ask him if he wants two or three spoons of mash.'

I mutter 'two or three, two or three' to try to remember as I go to the living room.

Tim is watching TV, singing along with dancing pigs. I suddenly see the time. It's five forty.

Mum! Where is she?

Tim sings louder. Grandad shouts, 'What did he say?'

To what? I can't remember what I was supposed to ask. I can't think of anything but Mum. Where is she? Why is she late? My tummy spirals in panic.

'Annie?' Grandad calls.

I shut my eyes but it doesn't stop. The spiral becomes a whirlwind. Tim keeps singing.

I'm scared. There's too much noise. My feet feel stuck to the floor, glued to the spot.

My brain goes 'MumMumMumMumMumMum' over and over again.

The whirlwind becomes a tornado.

The tornado lifts me up and pushes me out of the

room, my feet running down the hall, out the front door, crunching and racing down the gravel drive, onto the street, to the end of the road and across...

A car screeches to a stop. Bright-white headlights dazzle and pin me to the middle of the road.

A door opens.

'Annie? What are you...?'

It's Mum.

And the tornado stills, and I sink to the ground as Mum reaches me and takes my hand, and I can hear Grandad's rough voice calling from far behind.

There's a lot of shouting when we all get into the house, but not from me – I can't speak. Finally, Mum stops yelling and gives me a hug. I curl up in a ball as she rubs my back. Echo creeps closer now things are quieter and sticks his head under my arm. I stroke his soft, brown, velvety ears against my cheek.

'I'm not really cross. You just scared me, Annie. You can't run off like that.'

I can, I think. I did.

As if she can read my mind, Mum says, 'Okay, you can, but you shouldn't.'

I finally manage to speak. 'I had to get out, get away.'

'From what?' Her eyes are dark, and leaking tears, like they are filled with sadness.

I'm silent. I want to say, 'From the monster storm inside me. From my head and my body and everything that feels like it's going to explode.' But I don't. I don't want her to tell me I'm being silly, that my brain is all messed up. She doesn't ask any more. I breathe in and out in time with Echo.

We sit quietly in the living room while Grandad eats with Tim in the kitchen. Then Mum puts Tim to bed while I have dinner. The room is quiet. I look around at the walls, the furniture, the table, Echo curled up on his bed, my plate of food.

I am here, I think, and I am safe.

There's a little voice at the back of my mind that tries to shout out, 'Not for long, though!', but I do my best to ignore it. Everything feels sort of okay now.

CHAPTER TWO

I don't sleep well. Next-door's cat decides to have a yowling match with the tabby from down the road and it keeps me awake. In the morning, my eyes feel saggy and I can't think clearly while I'm getting dressed. It takes ages to put my buttons into the right holes.

At breakfast, I fidget. Something's not right, I

don't feel right. Tim is splashing cereal. I want to cut my toast into triangles but I get distracted by Tim's mess and do it into squares by mistake. I don't like food with four edges; three is much better.

'You can't have another piece, that's all there is.' Mum is speaking loudly. She might be cross. It might be because Tim is chattering away.

But I'm worried she might be cross.

I don't ask again, but I don't eat my toast.

'Stop wiggling, Annie.' Grandad puts his hand on my shoulder as I shuffle back and forth on the seat.

It's not a wiggle of choice. I'd rather sit still, but something is itchy-tickling me and I can't work out what.

They finally give up trying to get me to eat, and I go to put on my school shoes. I find my tights are the right way round, which is the wrong way round for me. I need them inside out so the tufty stitching bit isn't nibbling at my toes. So that's what was bothering me.

I put them on properly and immediately feel a lot better. I could even manage some square toast, but Grandad is pushing me out the door saying that we'll be late.

'I'm hungry.'

Grandad tells me it's my own fault for not eating breakfast. It's true, but I can't even begin to explain why it was that I couldn't.

My tummy starts opening up, becoming a cave. It's going to be a long wait until break time. I hate being really hungry. It makes me worry I will fold into myself and disappear.

School starts with assembly. As we are walking in I see Oscar with his infant class. He waves at me and I wave back. I am Oscar's playground buddy who helps him not feel lost or scared or worried. He's only little, but he's a great friend to have and he makes me laugh. I like seeing him and knowing he's okay. It's nice to share a wave.

Assembly begins. The floor is hard and makes my legs go to sleep. Our head teacher, Mrs Grevins, talks on and on and on about some important visitors coming tomorrow and how we all need to make sure we are wearing the proper uniform and following the school rules.

My head starts to droop. What she is saying is very boring and I am still sleepy because of last night. I also don't have any energy because I haven't eaten breakfast and my tummy hole is growing. I must stay awake, though. I remember times when Mrs Grevins was droning on but then suddenly noticed

Lily talking to Jasmine, or Finlay poking Tom, or William fidgeting. When she notices things she ROARS louder than a dinosaur. It makes me nervous that she might shout at me. I know I won't talk to anyone, but what if I don't look awake enough? Or I move because I'm uncomfortable?

The more awake I try to be, the more asleep I feel. Then I see my tights. They are perfect for me, but they aren't perfect for Mrs Grevins. They are inside out and not proper school uniform. That is going against the rules she is telling us are so important.

What do I do?

If I change them, my feet will be mad at me, and that will make my thoughts go all spikey and distracted.

If I leave them just right, Mrs Grevins will shout at me in front of everyone.

If she does that, my class will laugh, then the whole school will laugh. And then I'll cry, and then she'll be more cross and send me to her office, and she might call Mum and tell her I have to go home and that she won't let me back to school until I am wearing the tights properly. And then I can never go back.

The thoughts whistle back and forth, rockets shooting across my brain. I can't breathe. I can breathe. I can't breathe. My chest is tight and knotted and I don't know what to do. I rub my fingers together, pretending they are stroking Echo's ears, but I can't imagine the soft feeling well enough.

Then I realise everyone around me has stood up and is walking back to lessons.

'Hurry up, Annie!' Mrs Grevins calls.

I quickly jump up and rush to join my class.

'No running, Annie!' Mrs Grevins shouts.

I jolt to a stop. I can't run, so I can't catch up. I can't catch up and I can't join the class. It is impossible to do the right thing. And she is shouting and it is too loud and the worst thing is happening. Everything is going as wrong, as I imagined.

She comes up behind me and her voice takes up all the space in my head as it booms 'walk, you silly girl.'

My heart hurts and my eyes prickle. The tears feel like needles. I don't want to cry in front of her, in front of anyone.

CHAPTER THREE

Back in the classroom, I have to blink hard as we start working on maths. I will not cry. The numbers keep going blurry and I take my glasses off and clean them furiously, as if that will make my eyes see better. It doesn't really help, but it gives me something to do.

I wish Miss Jerris was here, but she's working with

Matthew today and I don't want to call her over. When Miss Jerris sits by me, I'm like the calm sea washing back and forth. I can work without big storms rising up.

My brain seems to have forgotten how to do multiplication. I recognise the numbers, but they won't calculate properly. I try to count on my fingers, but Harry spots me and mouths 'baby'.

I have to sit next to Harry, and he is always mean, but he doesn't want Mr Newman or Miss Jerris to know, so he hides it. He kicks me under the table and calls me names in whispers.

I try to ignore him. Mr Newman comes up behind us and looks at our work. Harry has nearly finished. I'm only on the third sum.

'Come on, Annie, this isn't like you. You need to speed up a bit.'

How can I speed up when I can't get the questions right? My brain is going as fast as it can, but it's not fast enough. I'm not good enough. I'm never going to finish this. I'm useless.

At break time I still haven't finished, but Mr Newman lets me go outside. Miss Jerris catches me as I'm putting my coat on.

'Annie, is everything okay? Are you alright?'

No, it's not. I'm not. But I don't know how to find the words to explain. I do an awkward nod-shake-shrug thing and Miss Jerris squeezes my arm. Her hand is warm.

She doesn't need to say anything else. I know she understands that I can't always put things into words. Just her touch gives me a bit of reassurance that I am not alone and some of the knots in my tummy loosen.

In the playground, I find Oscar sitting on the little low fence, swinging his legs and eating an apple. It's where he always waits for me. I perch by him and we swing our legs in time together. I eat an apple too. It's so good to have something fill my tummy. Each bite makes the hole get smaller. Oscar always eats one side of his apple first, and then the other. I eat all the way around in a spiral until only the bottom is left. We tried out each other's method but neither of us thought it was better. Sometimes we have a race to see who can eat their apple first, or who can finish last. Today we just sit and swing.

Oscar is quiet and likes looking at everything going on. He gets a bit scared of the bigger boys and girls, particularly if they are running around everywhere.

I wait for Oscar to speak first. It's nice to be with

someone with whom I don't have to force my words out.

'I've got games next.' He is very quiet and I look over. His head is pointing down to the ground and he has stopped swinging. I don't think he is happy. I know Oscar doesn't always like games.

'What are you worried about?'

'That I'll fall over. Or they'll pick me absolutely last. Or I'll get hit with a ball. Or I'll trip over a rope. Or...'

Oscar thinks a bit like me. We both go into catastrophes. It is easier for me to help him with his thoughts than help myself.

'Oscar, those things might happen, but even if they do, you will be alright. You can tell Mrs Hobbes, or you can come and tell me at lunchtime.'

'Okay.'

'And you know you like doing jumps and somersaults on the mats. So games is a good thing too.'

'I like handstands best.'

'So see how many you can do today, and come and tell me later.'

He smiles at me. The bell rings and we both throw our apple cores in the bin and go to our classrooms.

It was good to make Oscar cheery. It makes me feel a bit cheerier myself.

Maths was bad but geography is worse. Mr Newman is at the board showing us how the movement of the Earth's plates created all of the countries. Every time he talks about plates colliding and causing land to rise up, or turn into earthquakes or volcanos, Harry kicks me. I count the kicks – four…five…six – and I'm going to explode – eight…

nine…ten – and suddenly I can't stand it anymore.

I can't be here. I can't do this. I could run or shout or kick him back or…or…or…

I stop.

My head goes bang on my desk. I hear the blood rushing around in my skull. My eyes are shut, and I push my fingers against them, watching the stars and kaleidoscope colours I create. Harry has gone. Mr Newman has gone. I am gone.

Then a loud whack makes me present again. A steam train of sound rushes in. Harry is whispering to Ben, who sits in front of us. I open one eye and see Mr Newman's big, bony hand next to my face.

'Annie? Annie!' There's a sharp edge to his voice.

I shut my eye.

'Annie, sit up.'

I shake my head.

'Come on. Stop being silly. It's time for work.'

I don't move. I'm not being silly, I'm being sensible. I've had enough. If I shut myself away then I won't shout or yell or explode at Harry and make a scene. If Mr Newman would let me stay here quietly, no one would really notice. He's the one making a fuss.

I keep my head down. Harry's whispers are a snake, curling around me, tying me up tight. I want to block my ears but I'm frozen in place.

Mr Newman gives up. I look into myself and drift away in my mind, somewhere else, somewhere safe. I go to the beach and lie on the shore. There is nothing but me and the sand and the waves and the sky.

Finally, the bell rings and I am back in the classroom. I hear lots of clattering feet and bags. I smell the scents coming from the dinner hall. When all the feet seem to have stopped, I put my head up.

Mr Newman's blue shirt and grey tie hang in front of me.

'Mrs Grevin's office. Now.'

I keep my head low as I pick up my bag and drag myself out of the room.

CHAPTER FOUR

Grandad picks me up with Tim. I come out of the school front door instead of my classroom.

'What have you been up to today?' he asks. I think he must know something's happened but he doesn't ask anything else. He raises one eyebrow, which usually makes me laugh, but I can't laugh.

I have been sitting outside Mrs Grevins' office

since twelve thirty. She told me that if I wasn't going to be part of the class, I'd have to stay out of the class. It sounded good to me, but I knew it was a punishment. Only children who are naughty get sent to the head teacher, so I must have been bad.

I haven't eaten any more food because I didn't want to see anyone in the dinner hall. The only good bit was when Oscar came up to the window during lunch and waved. He mouthed 'eight' at me and mimed standing on his head by tipping himself sideways, and I clapped at him for doing so many. He beckoned for me to come out and play, but I mouthed 'no'. His smile went away and he hung his head. I wanted so much to go out to him, but I didn't have the energy to move.

Now I feel weak and worn out, like a rag that has been wrung too tight. My tummy hole has caved in on itself, crumpled down and given up on ever getting fed.

I don't say anything.

Grandad takes my hand and gives me Echo's lead and we all walk to the beach.

Tim runs to the edge of the water and starts piling up a sandcastle, as usual. Grandad helps him scoop a moat. I mooch among the rocks, then perch on the edge of a boulder, looking out to sea. Echo is dancing in the waves, the water bright and sparkly in droplets on his fur. The foam gives him a little beard when he dips his face in. I watch Echo play and I can feel my muscles begin to relax.

Barnacles bite my skin. They are knobbly and prickly and leave a funny, tiny star shape if I press my hand onto them. The air smells salty and a bit like old boiled cabbage; there's a lot of brown and green seaweed piled by the high-tide line.

Echo trots up. He sits on his haunches and stares at me, his face a big doggy grin of love, tongue lolling out of the side of his mouth. I jump down and we have a huge soggy, sandy cuddle. He lies on his back and I give his tummy a scratch as his tail wags away. His eyes are shut and I know he's happy. Seeing how my touch, my being there, makes Echo feel good gives me a warm tingle in my chest and face, and I realise I am smiling too.

'Echo, you are the best dog ever,' I whisper in his ear.

He sits up and sniffs my hands, then looks at me. I think he's saying I'm his best person ever.

I'm not always good. I don't always get things right. But for Echo what's important is that I'm there for him, like he is for me.

'Echo, I wish I could be as free as I am with you all of the time.'

He considers my words, then licks my hand. I'm not sure he has an answer, and maybe there isn't one. Maybe what's important is simply that we're here together, right now.

Echo scrabbles in the sand at my feet. I pick up a handful. It's damp and takes on the shape of my fist. I do it again and again, building up a pile of fist shapes. When I hold one in my hand, I can feel a million grains, tiny individual dots that I push and squash together until I have a solid mass. The pressure as I squeeze goes tingling all the way up my arm to my shoulder and behind my eyes. As I let the sand go, some of the pressure in my head goes too. When I have a good-sized pile of handfuls, I stamp it flat, squashing them all into the ground, turning them back into the beach again. And Echo and I leave together.

Tonight, Mum is home at her normal time and we all eat dinner together. Tim doesn't whine when he's asked to eat all of his pasta before he can have a pudding. Grandad remembers to put my pasta sauce in a separate bowl. If it's all mixed in together, there are too many flavours and textures to manage and it makes me stop being hungry. I have two helpings and eat it all up. I let Echo lick the bowl at the end.

I do some colouring with Tim before he goes to bed and then I read my favourite book. I am off flying with dragons, through the skies and up to the stars. I can picture myself there, clinging on to my dragon's red, scaly back, hearing the rushing whistle of wings as they pull us in huge, swooping loops.

'Bedtime, Annie.'

I jump as Mum comes into the room and am back with a bump, lying on the carpet.

'You need to have a shower tonight.'

A shower. I usually have a bath.

'Why?'

'Because I accidentally left the hot water tap on and there isn't enough water.'

'But I can't have a shower.'

'You can.' Her mouth is in a straight line and her eyes aren't crinkly round the edges like they get when she's happy.

I think: I can have a shower, but I don't want to. The water is like needles. My legs and arms get all hot then cold then hot again as they go in and out of the spray. Drops flick in my eyes. My feet aren't good at staying stuck to the floor and slip all over the place. I hate showers.

I have a brainwave. 'We can boil kettles of water and fill the bath!'

'If we want to be here all night…Nope, no way. Shower and bed. It won't kill you this once.'

It won't kill me, but it won't make me feel good. I don't like being unbalanced, being made all uncomfortable. It's tiring feeling all the different temperatures at once. I can just imagine it. My skin crawls with a thousand itchy thoughts and I shiver.

'Annie. Now.'

No, no, no, no. She can't make me. I won't. I don't want to feel that horrible. Today has had too much bad stuff in it already.

'No.'

I stare at the corner of my book, trying to magic myself back with my dragons.

'Annie...' I recognise the warning note in her voice. This could lead to shouting.

If I have a shower, I will feel horrible. If I don't, she will be mad and I will feel horrible in another way. Which is worse?

'Please?' Mum doesn't usually say please. It surprises me into looking at her. There is the sad face again, the dark eyes, and they are too much.

'Okay.'

I say it before I can think about it and get too scared. I go upstairs, into the bathroom. Clothes off, water on, under the shower, soap and shampoo, out and towel-dry, pyjamas and into bed. I mutter 'do it, do it' over and over under my breath, trying to keep myself functioning and not feeling.

It takes minutes, but it feels like forever. Echo comes and licks my face as I am drying off, which makes me wet again but also makes my skin feel more like my own. Finally, I'm in my room, lights off, the soft glow under the door, my head on the pillow. I'm so, so tired, I want to sleep for days. My limbs are heavy with the exhaustion of managing all of the sensations they've just been through. However much I try to tell myself otherwise, I can't stop feeling.

It takes hours for the feelings to fade and for me to relax into sleep.

CHAPTER FIVE

Tim is my daily alarm clock. He runs in at seven and climbs on me, patting my face with his hand, making his toy rabbit bounce on my head. We usually snuggle for a few minutes, taking Rabbit on adventures across the Land of Bed.

Today I push him away. He keeps boinging back like a spring, so I shove him and he falls to the floor with a cry. I want to reach down and give him an 'I'm sorry' hug, but I can't make myself move. He runs off to Mum.

Mum comes in. She is half-dressed for work and her jumper is the zigzag one I hate as the green and blue pattern stings my eyes. She stands right over me, talking loudly. My ears and eyes hurt and I roll over to face the wall. The paint is a tiny bit bumpy; I can see the popped air bubbles in the yellow surface. I count the dimples, then my vision blurs.

I realise Mum is shaking my shoulder. Her voice is really noisy now. I think I stopped hearing her tell me off.

She goes away and I tuck my head under my duvet. This space is warm and dark and quiet. It is mine and I am on my own. I want to call Echo to come up but I don't want to stop the silence in this space. I think Echo can read my mind when I am with him, but we haven't learnt to communicate when we're apart.

The quiet is over too soon. Big footsteps march in and stop. It will be Grandad. He doesn't often tell me off, but when he does I know I'm in real trouble. I stay very, very still. Perhaps Grandad will think I'm sick. But I am tense while I wait. I don't know what he's going to do.

I know I have to go to school, but I don't want to go because I don't want to make everything worse today. Yesterday I tried to do it right, and still ended up with Mrs Grevins. I couldn't talk to anyone, and then in the evening I was made to have a horrible shower. Today the special visitors are coming to school, and so I have to know how to behave and I have to wear my tights correctly. Just the thought of the tights makes me want to rip my feet off with how overwhelming they'll feel.

Even if I try to follow the rules and instructions and do and say what people expect me to, I might get it wrong again, and then what will happen? Will Mrs Grevins shout and send me home? Will Mum get really sad and mad? What does that make me?

I'm scared.

Everyone will think I'm a really bad person. And if they think it, that might mean I *am* a really bad person.

It makes sense that if I stay home, none of this can happen. I won't have to make myself feel terrible wearing the tights, and I won't have to get badly told off for not behaving in the correct way.

I need to stay under my duvet so that I can't get confused and hurt and then become bad and make people sad.

Grandad walks out of the room.

I stay under the covers while I hear him and Mum muttering outside the door.

'Annie. Get. Up. Now.'

It's Mum's 'I'm really serious and if you don't do what I say I am going to make sure you regret it' voice. I can feel my tummy starting to knot.

I don't do it.

She says it again. Louder. The knots are double-knotting themselves. I'm losing myself and all I can feel inside is stress and fear. I'm so, so scared.

Mum steps into the room and gives a massive yell: 'Annie! Now!'

The knots snap, my brain pings and I scream at the top of my voice, 'EVERYBODY LEAVE ME ALONE.'

I'm so loud I hurt my own ears, and my duvet

cave that was safe is suddenly filled with my own crossness and isn't okay for me anymore. I leap out of bed, hands over my ears, and curl into the corner of my room, a tiny space between my desk and wardrobe.

'Leave me alone, leave me alone.'

I have my eyes shut, my arms and legs are squeezed by the hard wood of the furniture, and I am held in shape. It makes me feel safer. I stay there like that until I can find my body again, until I know where my hands and head and feet are.

Minutes pass. I hear soft padding across my carpet and then a warm bundle is by me. A deep breath goes in and out, pulsing up through my feet. Echo's fur is soft and tickly on my toes.

I open my eyes.

Echo is resting his head on his paws, big brown

eyes focusing on me. His eyes say, 'I love you. I am here.' They don't ask me for anything and I could look into them forever. But I see a shadow and raise my head. Mum is sitting on my bed. She's looking at me and I have to look away. I can see sadness in her eyes and the sadness makes my heart hurt.

Did I make her sad? Does that make me bad? I can feel the knots building again.

Then I see her arm reach out and stretch towards me. She doesn't touch my hand, but she's there for me. Echo's eyes give me reassurance. I slowly reach up and my hand grips hers.

We stay that way for some time.

'What do you need from me, Annie?' Mum's voice is gentle. It's an interesting question.

I need quiet. I need not to be sad. I need to feel safe.

'I need to be at home.' There's quiet. 'Please.'

'Can you tell me why?'

I don't know where to start. But I hear the words 'can you' and know they're not a command.

'No. No, I can't right now.' I need to straighten out the words and sentences, but I can't put enough together to even say this out loud. 'Please,' I say again, 'it's all too much today.'

'Too much...' she echoes and strokes my hand with her thumb. I lean into her and she holds me safe.

CHAPTER SIX

Mum and I take the day off. She calls school and says I'm sick with a headache. Then she calls her boss and tells her that I'm unwell and she can't come in. Usually, Grandad looks after Tim or me when we're ill. I want to ask her what's different about this time, but words are still hard to say out loud. The loudness that spilled out earlier made me so shocked, it takes time to trust it won't happen again. Grandad takes Tim to nursery and the house is quiet.

Sometimes it feels like words have to travel miles and miles from my brain to my mouth, and I wait so long for the words to get there that I'm not sure of the point, so then I just give up. This isn't ideal, though, as it means my questions don't get answered, and then I start worrying about what the answers might be. So then there's even more going on in my head and all of the thoughts get crowded. At the moment it's a bit of a swamp of words.

Mum and Grandad check I'm okay to be left alone for a while. After I've spent some time cuddling Echo, I get dressed and go to find some food. It's very late for breakfast, but it is good to be in the kitchen, just me and Echo, who is now resting on his bed, chewing a rubber doughnut. There are no distractions, and this morning I do my toast in triangles as I like it. It tastes good. I can hold it by a point and nibble from the opposite one right up to my fingertips – then my hands don't get sticky and messy and I don't have to wipe them every few seconds, which takes ages and is irritating and tiring. Often so tiring I give up eating.

I chase some crumbs across the plate, building them into a pile, a crumb castle. It makes me think of the sand on the beach.

'Can we go to the beach?' I call out before I realise the idea is in my head. I can speak without pre-thinking the words when I am relaxed.

Grandad calls back, 'Boots and coat and then we'll be off.'

Boots, coat. Boots and coat.

My red boots are by the back door but my black

coat is not in the cupboard under the stairs. It's not behind the back door. It's not hanging on a chair. It's not in my bedroom.

I don't know where it is.

'Annie, come on.' Grandad is all dressed and waiting by the front door.

I can't, I can't leave until I have my coat. He told me to find my coat.

I hunt under Tim's jacket, under the chairs in the kitchen. It's not anywhere.

I have to have my coat.

'Annie!' He's standing with his arms folded. He's cross. I'm bad. I'm trying to be good and do what he says, but I've done things wrong. Again.

I didn't want to go to school because I thought I would get it wrong there.

Now I've got it wrong at home too.

I'm useless. I can't do anything.

I'm in the kitchen and Grandad's by the front door. There's nowhere for me to run to. Mum is on the stairs, so I can't escape to my bedroom and shut myself away. I'm stuck and I'm trapped – and then one moment I'm gripping the kitchen chair, and the next it's not there, it's across the room, on its back, and there's a big grey mark on the bright-white wall.

I'm really, really bad now. The world freezes for a second.

Then that tornado rises completely and spits me up and out and I am throwing myself towards the front door to escape. I will push myself through anything and anyone to get out of here.

Grandad and Mum have me by my arms and I am pulling and tugging and trying to get free. They hold on, they won't let me get to the door, and I am fighting and fighting – and then I see my hands, all red and clenched and tight, and I feel how much they ache.

The hurt from my hands spreads into my arms and shoulders and head and back and down to my tummy, where it turns itself into tears. The tears rise up and fall from my eyes. I drop to my knees and can't battle anymore. My head is down on the carpet and I think I will cry and cry and cry until I am all dissolved and gone.

Mum sits and holds my feet. Grandad has my shoulders. Their grip is loose; they're holding me in comfort now, not to keep me contained. Echo rests by my left knee. Everyone is quiet and they wait with me. My tears gradually stop, and I can feel their hands and paws. Their touch means I am still here.

I turn and look up at the ceiling. It's blue like the sky. Like the sky over the sea, the beach.

'I'm sorry I'm so bad.'

There's a moment of quiet. I don't know what they are going to say. If they agree that I am bad, I don't know what I will do with myself.

'You're not bad, you're Annie.' Grandad is talking, not shouting.

'And we love you.' Mum is talking too.

No shouting means they're not cross.

She carries on. 'We love you, but we want to understand.'

Where do I start? How can I begin to explain how my worries, my thoughts, all jumble up and hurt my head? How I don't know what to do at times, and I get scared, and then panic that my fear is wrong and that I am bad. How I feel so sad or terrified or anxious that I think it will take over my heart and head and body so they're not even mine anymore and I don't know how they will behave. How I'm scared of myself, because I don't know how to be me without everything in the world seeming too much to cope with.

I don't know where to start making all that make sense, so I end up saying all my thoughts hodgepodge. Mum has found my coat balled up in my school rucksack and we have walked down to the beach and all the way up to the far end of the flat sand where the jagged grey cliffs rise to the clouds. We are drawing pictures in the sand with driftwood, and I track wiggles along the line of the last high tide as I let my words spill out. The sand oozes up brown water the deeper I dig down.

Mum and Grandad let me talk without

interrupting. I think I am saying everything aloud but I repeat some of it just in case I've actually been talking in my head. There are a lot of words to say and I feel like I have spilled out a huge book by the time they gradually slow and stop.

I look down. My wavy lines are huge, deep gouges. Puddles of water pool at the bottom. Grandad has been drawing boats and fish. Mum's picture is just a big letter A. Echo hasn't been drawing but his paw prints are dotted in between, linking us up.

'Is that A for Annie?' I ask.

'Who else?' She smiles at me, but her eyes are wet. She has been crying. I have made her sad and made her cry again.

My arms become hard sticks like the driftwood I am holding.

She does that thing where I wonder if she can read my mind.

'No, I'm not sad or upset with you.' My arms shake loose. 'I'm sad *for* you.'

Sad for me? That's a bit different. Mum explains that it means she is sad about what I've said because she knows I'm hurting.

She has understood some of me.

'So what I said makes sense?' I am excited. Maybe it seems all muddled to me but really other people feel exactly the same.

Mum pauses.

'I can't understand everything. That's not because it's wrong or it's not true. It's because we're different people.'

Grandad joins in. 'We're not going to feel everything in the same way that you do. But the more we can hear about how the world is for you, how you experience it, the better we can be with you in it.'

The sudden excitement has dropped away. I feel a bit alone now, as if no one is ever going to be with me, right in my space. But I think about how I don't like people crowding in, and that a little bit of room might be just right. Then Echo is there, nose in my hand, tail thumping against my leg. Echo understands me without words. I know he is there and that I am here and we are together even when we are apart.

'Can you help us be with you?'

I look at Grandad. 'What does that mean?'

'It means trying to tell us or show us when you have a big feeling, something that seems like it might take you over.'

'And,' says Mum, 'it means us working together to find a plan to help you manage those big feelings too. So that even if they don't always feel very comfortable, you know how to be with them.'

'You can look after me by helping me to look after myself?'

'That's pretty much it.' Grandad leans back and throws his stick far out into the sea. It bobs around until I can't see whether it's floating off or sinking.

I think about what they have said. I don't have to change me, but if I can feel better about who I am, maybe I won't get so confused and stressed that I want to explode or run away or disappear from everything. Maybe I can be okay.

CHAPTER SEVEN

Grandad and Mum and I have walked up to the promenade and are sitting together on a bench. We're eating chips, and seagulls are creeping near in the hope of leftovers. The sky is all blue and grey and tinged with pink where the sun is beginning to dip down in the spring afternoon.

'That's the colour of the thought spirals that come

into my head.' I point out a big silver-grey cloud that hangs low over the water. 'The pink is when I see Tim giggling.'

'And the blue?' asks Mum.

I ponder. 'The blue is when I take a deep breath just before I do something scary.'

'When you're building up your courage?'

I nod yes. My mouth is full of happiness and chips. The hot potato warms my tongue and throat. Vinegar smells tickle my nose. The chips make my face feel good.

As we watch, the cloud is spread out by the wind, the curves flattened and pulled apart, puffs wisping off sideways. In a few minutes, it's like it was barely even there.

'Annie, you've just described your feelings really clearly to us.'

I consider. Mum's right. I have. When I link my feelings to colours, I can find the words better, I can understand. Then I am clearer about what's going on.

'Could you do this more?' she asks.

It's very new, and quite strange. What if I can't do it again and I fail at it – fail at yet another thing? 'I don't know.' I really don't.

Grandad puts his hand on mine. 'But how about trying?'

I worry that when I get stressed I won't remember to find colours or won't be able to.

'Mum and I can prompt you. If you can let us know things are starting to build up, we can say the word "colour" to you.'

'I like that idea.' I will still be in control but I won't be on my own. 'Okay. I'll try. But promise you won't get mad if I can't?'

Mum takes my other hand. 'We won't get mad.'

Grandad also promises and I let my hands stay still with theirs. Echo looks up at me and his eyes tell me he will never, ever be mad. He will always be there.

Later, before dinner, Tim is dancing around the kitchen, banging a fork on the table and tins and drawers and the sink.

I put my hands over my ears.

'Annie, play with me. Play with me. PLAY WITH ME!' he shouts.

My hands turn into fists.

'Colour,' Grandad says softly.

I try to concentrate through the noise. The din goes on and on as Grandad tries to quieten Tim down. I see the inside of my head, green and dark like old seaweed. I am filled with deep, dusky emerald. Seaweed can be dried in the sun, can be blown away in the sea breeze. I breathe in and out, in and out. As I exhale, the colour starts to push apart; I can see faint lines of white light between.

I breathe again, in and out.

The spaces are bigger. The green colour is there, but there's a shimmering in between.

In and out again, and now the solid colour has become small, glittery dots.

With a final breath, I imagine blowing all of the green glitter out and away and off into the sky, where it can drift in the wind, scatter in the sea and dance along the sand.

I open my eyes and the colour is gone. Tim is sitting playing with Echo, and Grandad is stirring soup.

He raises an eyebrow in a question. I grin at him. The green, the overwhelming chaos of noise, is gone. I skip off upstairs light as sea foam.

CHAPTER EIGHT

I wake up early, and I know I have to go to school today. I can't have another day off. I have to face Mrs Grevins, Harry and Mr Newman. I don't want to. I can't, I think. I know that I have to and I need to, but it's not Miss Jerris's day to work with me, and I don't want to get through it on my own.

The panic starts to build up from my toes to my

knees to my tummy. It spreads through me, freezing me solid. I am a block of ice. I cannot move; I cannot feel anything but the heavy, deep cold.

I think of icebergs. I think of the TV programme about the Arctic I watched a few weeks ago. I remember the dazzling white of the frozen ice, the sharp bright-blue of the jagged edges.

I picture myself shining turquoise. I imagine myself floating in the ocean.

And I breathe, in and out, and I break the colour down. I am small ice pieces caught on the sea's flow. Then tiny chunks bobbing along. And finally, I've melted down into the water.

I open my eyes. Echo bounces in, soon followed by Tim and Rabbit, and I am warm and alive and I reach for them and smile.

The hours until break time go smoothly enough.

There is assembly and I look for Oscar but cannot see him. He is not here today. My head starts firing off in a million different directions about whether he is sick or sad or I upset him or he's away on holiday, but I pinch my toes to pull myself back and focus on Mrs Grevin's voice. I don't want to get told off for not paying attention. A little voice says 'Oscar, Oscar, Oscar' in my head, and I don't forget him, but I don't think about the what-ifs or whys either.

I survive our spelling test and our dictation without Harry saying anything to me at all. He might be ignoring me, and if so, he's doing me a favour, because it lets me think about the language and words and my pen on the paper. I get eighteen out of twenty and feel almost pleased. I wish I'd got them all right. I don't want to be perfect, I just don't want to get things wrong.

At playtime I hunt for Oscar, but he's definitely not here. I work out the words and finally manage to ask Daniel from his class, who tells me that Oscar's sick. I hope he's not really ill.

I wander around the edge of the playground and send Oscar silent get-well messages. I don't like to think of him poorly, as I know how horrid it is.

I stop with a bump as Katy, Lara and Hannah stand in front of me. 'Annie, where have you been? We need you for our game!'

Katy and Lara and Hannah are in my class. Katy and Lara are best friends and worst enemies – not at the same time, but most days they seem to switch. Hannah is friends with both of them, or neither when they ignore her if they're being mean.

I'm sort of friends with all of them, but I'm not really in their group. I like Katy because she's funny and pulls faces and does impressions of the teachers, but she always wants attention and I don't always have the energy to give it. I like Lara and Hannah because they're gentle and are happy to be quiet and sit reading books with me. They're easier to be with without Katy, but she always seems to be there.

I find being with them confusing too. I can't work out why you'd be mean to someone one day and then hug and squeal with them the next. I don't know what makes someone say they're your best friend but then send a mean note about you to other girls.

So I like spending time with them sometimes, but I don't always trust them. It's easier to sit and watch than it is to get involved.

Lara links her arm with mine and tugs me over to the two big beech trees. The rotten leaves from autumn are all smooshed on the ground and Hannah kicks the clumps apart. Katy is asking me what I watched on TV last night, and I'm about to say I didn't watch anything, but she's not really wanting an answer as she goes straight into telling me all about her favourite actor.

'Annie? Annie! Don't you like that movie too?' I realise she's asked me another question, but this time I was supposed to say something.

What did she ask? I screw my eyes up, but then Katy suddenly changes the subject and orders us all into a very complicated game of tag. I can't follow what she's saying but I figure I'll just copy the others when we start. Then there's a very, very long rhyme to pick the person who is It.

I'm It. Again. Somehow it's always me. I hate being It. Although at least I know what to do in this role.

So I start running after Lara, as I know she is the slowest. She stands on a tree root just as I tap her shoulder and call, 'It.'

'No, I'm safe.'

'You're not touching anything!' I'm very confused. Usually, safety is a tree trunk or bench or wall.

'Katy said any bit of the tree is safe today.'

So again we all run around and up and down, and finally I tap Katy. 'It!' I stop, panting; my chest is tight.

'I'm safe.' She pouts and crosses her arms.

I examine her. 'You're not on a root or touching the trunk. You're It.'

'I'm on the leaves, silly.' She throws her head back and laughs. 'Keep going.'

I look around. This is ridiculous. We are under the beech trees and there are leaves and twigs and beech nuts everywhere. I will never win. I will always be trapped. I tell Katy it's not fair and we need to play somewhere else.

She says no. I hurt. My chest hurts. My face hurts. I feel tricked and stuck.

Then Hannah chips in and backs me up. 'Come on, Katy. Annie's right. It's not fair.'

Katy moves forward, into the space around me that's mine. She's right up close and I can see the freckles on her nose, the flash in her dark eyes. I want to step back, but this is my space, it's mine, and she shouldn't be here. My hand rises – and the whistle shrieks for the end of break.

It snaps Katy back and she steps away, calling for Lara. They run towards the classroom.

Hannah pats my shoulder. 'You know Katy and her stupid games. Ignore her.'

She is being kind and I know I need to show her that I hear her. I sigh and pat her own arm back. There is a moment between us where I imagine that we'd both like to break free from Katy, and maybe we could, together.

Then the whistle goes again and the moment is lost for now, but we walk back together and I think that it's nice to have Hannah as a friend. There's a bit in my tummy, though, that is brittle, like one of the few dried leaves left on the tree. It's just holding itself together, but even the slightest shock might make it shatter into dust. Moments with Katy often leave me like this.

CHAPTER NINE

Harry keeps elbowing me in class. We are supposed to be drawing the lifecycle of a frog, but his jiggling means my tadpoles are all squiggly and I can't get the legs of my frog to bend in the right place.

'Stupid Annie. You can't add up, and you can't even draw a straight line.'

I am drawing an arrow and he makes my pencil jerk in the wrong direction.

I try to ignore him and concentrate, but there's a lot of chattering in the classroom. It's hard to block out the other conversations and Harry's teasing and only think about my work.

I can't hold my hands over my ears and draw at the same time. I keep a hand on my right ear, but it's not enough, and Harry is on my left side.

'Stupid, stupid, stupid.' Harry is sing-song muttering under his breath as he draws a perfect piece of pond weed.

There is too much noise. I am tight and hot and cold and shattering all at once.

The leaf inside me is powder. I can't find a colour anymore. I can't find my thoughts that will make me feel better. I don't know who I am – I just know I'm feeling all wrong.

My hand clenches around my ruler. The edges bite into my palm and fingers. It's not enough to focus my brain. I want to hit him, but I know that will get me sent out of the room. I can't, I can't be bad today.

But I can't find my colour. I can't find anything.

Harry pokes me again, and before I can stop myself I jab his book hard. I can see my arm rising up and coming down in slow motion, but I can't stop it. It's as if I'm in a dream until it whacks, and then all of the sound and noise and movement comes into my brain in a whoosh. Everything is outside of me in this moment and I am filled with relief that I have stopped him, like I have erupted all my anger away.

The corner of the ruler has ripped a hole right through his diagram. I feel so terribly bad. There is a sickness running through me, like I am rotten right down to my middle.

Then I sit absolutely still and wait for the consequences to begin.

Harry is immediately on his feet. 'Mr Newman, Mr Newman.' He is waving his hand in the air and jumping up and down on the spot.

I put my head down on the desk with a hard smack and shut my eyes.

'Annie's ripped my work! It's not fair!' Harry sounds indignant. I am numb.

Mr Newman is suddenly beside me. It startles me and I sit up. My head is throbbing and I can feel tears prickling my eyes.

'It's no good crying now, Annie. You can't pick on Harry like this.'

The unfairness of the words stabs at me. I don't

pick on Harry, he picks on me. And I'm not crying over what I've done to him, I'm crying because I'm hurting. The tornado is swirling inside my chest, but it's a muddy mess of every colour turned into horrible sludge, and I can't find anything to focus on and that makes me scared as well.

'You don't know anything!' I shout at Mr Newman, and I am standing up now and about to run. But Mr Newman is right beside me and I can't escape.

The class has gone silent and everyone is staring. Miss Jerris walks over and I shut my eyes again and try to disappear. I hear Mr Newman step back and then her hand covers mine. She doesn't say anything, but instead of feeling that I am being pulled inside out, her touch keeps me more contained.

I open my eyes and stand up, and she slowly walks

me over to Mrs Grevin's office. What I was so scared of happening has happened all over again.

'It's okay, Annie,' Miss Jerris tells me before she has to go back to the classroom.

I want to believe her, but it's hard when I am on my own with someone who might roar. I want to ask her to stay with me, but I don't. My shouting has made me lose my words and my voice.

I am told to sit at the desk outside Mrs Grevin's door. I can hear her answer the phone. The sharp beeping sound rips through my brain; it tears holes in my thoughts. I won't do any work. I refuse to even open my book. Mrs Grevins says I'm sulky and stubborn.

I'm not sulking, I'm scared.

I'm scared I will get everything wrong, even more wrong than it already is.

I know there are colours in me somewhere but I can't find them, can't concentrate enough to work out what they are and where and why. As soon as I get a glimpse, all I can think is, I'm useless, and they whisk off and away.

Hannah comes and waves at me at lunch, like Oscar did the other day. I wave back, robotically. She does a little dance and I find my face feels lighter. Then Katy comes up from behind and yanks her off and away. Before she goes Hannah does a funny shrug and a smile, like 'What can I do?', and I wave at her again to try to show I understand.

The brightness goes. Hannah has gone. Oscar isn't here. Katy didn't even look at me or wave, and so I guess she must not really want to know me at all. And I want to not care but I do, because now I am sitting here feeling really lonely and I can't make myself feel safe.

I won't eat lunch. I won't talk. Mrs Grevins gives up and calls Mum.

I sit still as a rock and do not speak.

It's Grandad who walks through the front door. He does the eyebrow raise at me but I ignore him. Mrs Grevins takes him into her office and shuts the door. I can't hear words but I can hear the voices going back and forth. They are talking about me. I want to not care but I do. I can pretend to be stone but really my insides are soft and being ripped apart.

Grandad comes out. 'It's okay, Annie,' he says. Then he picks up my bag and coat, takes my hand and I go without looking back.

CHAPTER TEN

Grandad doesn't talk again the whole way to Tim's nursery. He doesn't say anything to me when Tim comes running out with Rabbit bouncing in his hand. He doesn't talk to me when we walk down to the beach. Echo looks up at me as he trots along. Each glance reminds me he is there and I am here. I can't concentrate on any more than that.

It is earlier than usual at the beach. There's no one around at all, and we have the whole place to ourselves.

I am convinced Grandad is mad at me. He must be furious to not talk to me all this time. He said he wouldn't be mad, but now he is.

I said I'd try, and I did try, but I couldn't find the colour. I don't know why it didn't happen. It's like this magic idea gave the illusion of helping me but then disappeared in a puff of smoke. It's almost worse than if it had never worked at all.

Echo darts off into the waves, pretending to chase the fat seagulls. He becomes like a puppy as soon as he is loose from his lead. I want to play with him but I have too many knots. I try to imagine playing with him but I can't picture myself. There's just a space where I should be.

I look down and see my fingers are picking at my skin again. It looks red. I seem to start digging at myself when I am lost, burrowing to find something. I can't feel the soreness that I know must be there somewhere. I know I should stop, but my hands won't obey my thoughts. I need to distract them so the hurt doesn't keep me awake tonight.

The rocks are scattered with empty, discarded shells from periwinkles and limpets and whelks. I choose a broken fragment and bash it to smithereens between two stones, grinding it down to fine powder. It feels good to break something. I find another, then another.

Shadows come over me, and I see Grandad and Tim standing there.

'Come on, Tim,' Grandad says. 'Let's form a smashing factory.'

He and Tim go off and hunt for empty shells. They bring me piles that I smash and crash to smithereens. I keep going for ages until I am covered with a gritty dust that tastes bitter on my tongue. There are plenty more shells, enough for smashing forever, but my arms are exhausted and they ache. I can feel my body, feel myself again, and it is time for home.

Grandad still hasn't spoken directly to me. Just as we're leaving the beach, he says quietly, 'Colour?'

I am pearly silver. The cool, shiny inside of a mussel shell, the quiet calm after fear has eased.

I don't say anything, but I think: I found it again.

Maybe the magic has not completely gone.

After Tim is in bed, Mum calls me into the kitchen. She has a small pile of pebbles and shells in front of her. I sit on a chair opposite.

'Pick the one that feels right.'

I find a shiny mussel shell, just like I imagined.

'Keep looking,' she says. 'What colours are there?'

I hold it up so it catches the light, glimmering peach and pink and cream. Turning it back over, I see the surface is almost indigo, with amethyst shades, and dusky greys and blues.

'The more colours you can see, the more choice you'll have. Every day, we'll come to the beach and you can find something there that holds the colours you've felt. If you bring the objects home, they will remind you of the beach, and they can also remind you of the colours you can find.'

I keep staring and I consider. My face aches from being still as stone and not showing feelings.

'I couldn't do it.' As I say it, I let go and am filled with a rushing heat and my eyes start crying. I didn't know there were tears inside. 'I tried and tried, but everything else filled my head too much for me to find the colour.'

'But that's okay. I mean, it's not okay you ruined Harry's work, but it's okay you can't always find the colour.'

'I want to.'

'I know. But you've just started. And nothing is ever perfect. Even when you've been doing this for months, there will still be moments when it is just too hard.'

Mum is saying it is alright to get things wrong sometimes. I don't think I really believe that with every part of me, but I trust that she does.

'Annie, this isn't going to be one quick fix. It's about finding all the bits and pieces you need. And that might take some time.'

'And even then, they might not always work. But that's okay?' I need to hear her reassurance clearly.

'That's okay.'

I have the idea of colours. I also have a little mussel shell that fits in my pocket. And now there will be a daily trip to the beach so I can measure how things have been.

I am learning how to do things differently.

CHAPTER ELEVEN

Mum had a chat with Mrs Grevins and now Miss Jerris is working with me for an extra day a week. It makes a big difference, but Harry is still mean to me three days out of five. That's a lot of days to put up with and I have to get good at finding colours on Mondays, Wednesdays and Fridays. There have been good days and bad days and better days again.

The bad days are muddy and muddly. I sometimes stop talking. I sometimes explode, although this only happens now at home. I haven't done anything to Harry or his work. I hold on and on and on all day.

Sometimes, I manage to find a shell or rock that's the perfect colour for how I've been. A sunrise grey or flecky black, a shiny cream that reflects the light. I can crash it to dust, hold it tight in my fist, or bury it in a massive sand pile that Tim helps me and Echo build. I can keep it or get rid of it as I need. I don't always want to take my colours home.

But on a bad day, the colours are impossible to find, and sometimes even the beach doesn't help. Echo's eyes gaze at me with love, but I can't look back. That's when I know I'm all lost and wrong.

When I finally get home, in my room where I

am safe, it all comes out. I shout at Tim or slam the door or throw my shoes against the wall. The noise sometimes shocks me back to feeling sad and hurt, but sometimes it's too late and I get told off and yelled at by Mum and Grandad, because they don't know, they can't know, how much I already hurt inside. How much I don't want to hurt them too.

It ends in a soggy cuddle, a heap of us tucked into one another, and Echo's steady breathing grounding me to the world. It ends with love, it ends with feeling release. I just wish I could get to the end without going through such fear first.

On the days when Miss Jerris works with me, I often feel a lot calmer. There's less buzzing in my brain, fewer knots in my tummy. At break times, I always catch up with Oscar, but I also join in with whatever Hannah and Lara and Katy are doing.

Sometimes they sit and talk about TV from the night before. I don't like TV much, particularly programmes where the story is all jumbled up and told to you in bits. They're really hard work to watch. I can't remember everyone's faces and names and it's a headache to work out the story. I used to pretend I understood to join in the conversation, but then Katy found me out and laughed. My face went hot, and Hannah quickly changed the subject to the dancing competition programme. I watch this, as it's easy to follow and I like all of the sparkly lights and costumes and music. I have lots to say. Katy used to love it, but now she says she's bored and doesn't want to talk about it anymore. I've heard her and Lara discussing the costumes and the dancers in class and at dinnertime, so I know she's lying, but I don't know why.

Other times we play tag, which is okay, although I'm still often the person who does the catching from the beginning. A game I like better is when we pretend that we're on secret missions. We stalk one of the lunchtime supervisors around and try not to be seen, or we make up codes with symbols and hand gestures so we can communicate in our own secret language. I could play these games for hours, and Lara and Hannah often tell me how good I am at pretending different missions and making up plans.

When Lara started saying this, Katy got all huffy and stopped talking. She deliberately dropped her bag, just as we'd nearly crept right up to Mrs Fisher by the dinner hall door, and Mrs Fisher turned and spotted us at once. After we ran away Katy started using a secret code to spell out my name and a very, very rude word. She said she wasn't but I saw, and

Lara giggled and I went all hot again, and then I couldn't speak. I managed to find a shiny black colour and focus on that. That afternoon I got a deep, dark piece of rotten seaweed and shredded it into tiny, tiny pieces that Echo and I threw into the churning tide.

The best days are when Lara and Katy are doing their own thing and Hannah and I make up stories just for the two of us. Or Hannah asks me about Echo and Tim. Or I ask her about her hamster called Cluedo and her older sister Beth who stays out late at night and makes their dad cross. The best, best days are when Oscar and Hannah and I sit on the benches and play cards or a guessing game, all of us quiet but doing something together. There's not very much talking, just the fun and the fresh air and the time with my friends.

Then Lara is ill for a few days. Katy starts paying lots of attention to Hannah and asking her over for tea after school and doing her hair in a new fancy style at lunchtimes. Oscar is scared of Katy, because she's loud around him and ignores that he's there. I want to carry on playing with Hannah, but I don't really want to play with Katy. And I definitely don't want to leave Oscar out.

So I split my lunchtime in half and do a bit of leg swinging and catching up with Oscar, then I go to find Katy and Hannah, who are plaiting grass by the edge of the field.

I sit cross-legged next to them and pick some grass of my own. Katy slightly shifts so her back is a bit towards me. Hannah smiles at me and carries on chatting to Katy. I can't follow what they are discussing so I focus on the grass. It's soft in my fingers, delicate. I run a blade against my cheek.

I am on my second plait before Katy gives me a glance. 'You're doing it all wrong.'

'No, I'm not!' I am indignant. I hold up my plaited grass, pale green and tightly woven. It's just as neat as hers, and neater than Hannah's.

'You are, isn't she, Hannah. You have to go right over left first, not left over right.'

That's ridiculous. It doesn't matter which way you start. I tell her so.

'Don't call me names. You're stupid, Annie James. Harry calls you stupid, I hear him. The whole class hears him. We all think you're stupid too. So does Mr Newman.'

Hannah tries to intervene. 'Katy, stop…'

Katy's head whips around and she stares at Hannah until she's quiet. Hannah's head drops, but she subtly moves one of her feet until it is touching mine. The foot keeps me connected, to Hannah and to myself. I know I have to think of colours or I am lost.

I can't stay here. I don't want to sit with Katy. I hate her, I hate how she always has to be better than everyone else. I feel stuck and I can't move, but I can't stay.

I focus for a moment. My inside is dark red like a squishy sea anemone stuck to the rock at the bottom of a pool. I imagine the seawater washing in and out, helping the anemone to feed and grow. I breathe with the sea flow.

And I stand up and leave and I think: I am okay, I have done okay.

CHAPTER TWELVE

I watch the sea anemones that afternoon. Prod
one with a finger, feel the jelly surface wobble at
my touch. I am wobbly too. I have people I like
to spend time with and people I don't, but I can't
always do one without the other. I was able to walk
away today, but I also walked away from someone
I like.

I'm quiet all evening. Mum tries to get me to tell her what's wrong, but all I can say is 'wobbly' and 'friends'. I can't put all of the other words in between to make more sense of it. She doesn't keep questioning me about it, though.

As I'm getting tucked into bed for the night, she asks if I'd like a surprise before school tomorrow.

'It depends.' Surprises can be good, or bad. Not knowing makes them a bit scary to contemplate.

'It involves the beach. And you and me.'

I think for a few moments.

'Okay. Yes, please.'

Mum wakes me up before Grandad or Tim are stirring. There's no light outside, not even the pale grey before the sun arrives. She mimes 'shhhh' at me, and I get dressed in my joggers and jumper, warm woolly socks and gloves and coat. Mum tugs a hat on my head and we get Echo and go out the door and walk down to the beach.

There's been a sharp frost overnight, so late in the spring I am surprised, and the daffodils and tulips in the gardens are all droopy under the weight of the ice. They look like they want to curl up to keep warm. The cold prickles my nose and makes my lips numb so I couldn't talk even if I wanted to.

We get to the beach just as the sky is growing pink. I can see the sand is perfect. We are the first ones here. There are no human footprints, just the webbed waddles left by a gull. But the sand is magical. Dusted with frost, it glows as the sun rises; it sparkles with a billion crystals of light, turning the beach into an enchanted carpet.

I dance off over it, Echo scampering alongside. I throw my arms out wide, flying across my beach –

my space, my amazing place. We stop for breath by the water's edge. The sea looks orange and blue and yellow and red and grey and green, and the white tops of tiny waves shimmer it all into a coloured haze.

I turn and see Mum back near the promenade. She waves. I wave my hands high in the air and spin and spin and spin until I am blurred with the colours, the crystals, the magic, and I am a part of the wonder and it is a part of me.

I spin until I fall down, and then I lie, watching as the sky becomes gradually more and more blue. Echo is on my legs, pinning me down.

I see Mum come into my vision. She holds out a hand, and I am a bit all over the place but I manage to get upright. We go home for breakfast and I keep hold of the magic in me.

CHAPTER THIRTEEN

As the weeks slip by I get better and find it easier to keep my colours. It's the first really warm day of summer today and the end of the week. That means a weekend of being just at home and on the beach. No stress from school and no people asking me to do things. If I can find my colours today, I will be okay.

Things start well. I have time for a game of running round the bushes in the garden with Echo before school. Grandad packs me triangle sandwiches for lunch, and I sit with Oscar and we talk about all the best fillings. He likes cheese and jam and peanut butter and sometimes he even has them all together. I pull a yukky face. I like lots of different foods but they need to be kept separate. I like Marmite. And cheese (but only Cheddar or Edam). And sometimes I like hummus, but not with white bread. But never, ever anything else with any of them. So Grandad cuts up tomato and lettuce and cucumber and puts them in little pots on the side. I prefer my food separate for all of my meals.

'Why don't you eat things together, Annie?' Oscar asks me as he is chewing a mouthful. He starts coughing and it takes me a bit of time to pat his back and get him a glass of water before he is quiet.

I don't usually like people asking me questions about food. People ask as if they're interested, but really they just want to tell you how you're doing it wrong compared to them. I don't mind questions from Oscar, though.

'Lots of foods mixed together is too much thinking for my tongue to work out all the flavours. Then I miss the different tastes.'

'Okay.'

And that's why I don't mind. Because Oscar wants to hear my answer but he doesn't want to analyse it, to criticise or judge. Other people seem to think that I should eat exactly as they do.

How I eat is how I eat and it shouldn't matter to anyone else. It doesn't matter to Oscar.

Harry is different.

He walks past on his way out to the playground.

'Stupid Annie. Can't eat normal sandwiches.'

I ignore him, but Oscar doesn't.

'Shush. You be quiet and leave Annie alone.' He is sitting bolt upright and his face is very red. Little Oscar is talking to one of the boys he finds really scary. He is doing it for me.

Harry opens his mouth but shuts it again. I don't think even he wants to be mean to little Oscar, so he just thumps me hard on the back and walks off.

Oscar jumps up and immediately starts rubbing the bit of my back where Harry hurt me. I am breathing really, really quickly, tight, tiny breaths of panic.

'It's okay, I'll make it better.' His voice is soft and his hand is small.

I think of a little shell, a tiny spiral held in my

palm. I think of the cream colour, peaceful and cool. I imagine two shells next to each other. Oscar was so brave, and his breath is trembling too.

I reach round and catch his hand. We don't say anything, but I hold on to him until I can hear our breaths calming together, in and out, even and slow.

It's the end of lunch. I don't want to leave Oscar, I don't want him to leave me. I remember the shells, think about finding them on the beach later.

'See you later.' I smile at him to let him know I'm okay.

'Alligator,' he says back. And grins too.

Maybe we're both telling each other what we want to hear. Maybe we are okay. We've been there for each other.

CHAPTER FOURTEEN

Harry is straight on at me when afternoon class starts. He mutters about my lunch, about how I look, and about how I only have Oscar as a friend.

'So?'

'So everyone knows that one friend means you're sad. Sad and boring and stupid and nobody likes you.'

Oscar likes me. Hannah likes me. Miss Jerris likes me. Mum and Grandad and Tim like me. And Echo loves me.

I ignore Harry.

'Oscar is a baby. A silly little boy.'

'He's not. He just gets scared about things sometimes.'

I can see my hands turning into balls. I can feel my chest getting hot. My face is tight. I am just about learning to ignore Harry when he's being mean to me, but I'll do anything to defend Oscar.

'Baby, baby, baby. Oscar is a baby.' And then Harry kicks me really hard.

I'm so full of rageful colours, I can't find one to concentrate on. I don't want to hit Harry, I don't, but I can feel my arm rise up like a puppet on a string and I don't know how to stop it – it feels beyond my control.

There's a cough from behind. My arm drops with a smack. We both turn. Miss Jerris is there. Her face is still and her eyes are flashing. She looks like she might roar like Mrs Grevins.

'Get up.'

Both Harry and I immediately stand up. My anger has vanished and I am now feeling so sick I think I will wobble over. I don't know what's going to happen, what she heard, what this means.

'Not you Annie.' I sit straight back down, my legs collapsing me onto the chair.

'Harry, come with me. You're going to tell Mrs Grevins exactly what has just happened.'

Harry starts to protest, but Miss Jerris raises one finger and he stops. They go out of the room. The class are looking at me until Mr Newman gets their attention by banging on the desk.

Harry doesn't come back.

I don't know if I am relieved. I worry about what he will say to Mrs Grevins, what will happen when he does come back and sit next to me again. What he will do next.

Did I do something wrong too?

My colours, I find, are all are blurry, in spots and flecks of different shades. I am reminded of the sand, the tiny bits of green and brown, of ochre, white and blue. It's all muddled up, but there is something there for me to concentrate on.

Miss Jerris and Mr Newman call me over at the end of the day.

'Annie, why didn't you tell me what Harry was doing?' Mr Newman is cross-sounding.

So I should have told him about Harry. But if I'd done that, Harry would have picked on me even more. I freeze at the thought I've made a mistake.

Miss Jerris seems to understand. 'It's alright Annie.' She turns to Mr Newman and interprets for me. 'I think that Annie didn't feel she could say anything. Is that right?'

I consider her words and then nod.

Mr Newman sighs. I sneak a glance at him and see he has that exasperated face with two raised eyebrows. He really doesn't get me. It makes me feel empty.

Then I look at Miss Jerris and she is smiling at me and her hands are reaching out towards me.

'I think it might be better for Annie if Harry was to move seats.'

Yes! That would be brilliant!

Mr Newman makes a decision. 'Okay, then I'll put Michael in his place.'

I freeze again. I don't want anyone to replace Harry. I don't want anyone there at all.

'Please…' I can't find the words. I look up at Miss Jerris.

'It might be easier for Annie if she could sit on her own.'

I nod enthusiastically, rapidly up and down.

Mr Newman turns away. 'Very well, you can sit on your own. But don't come complaining to me if you get lonely.'

You really, really don't get me, I think. Simply sitting by people doesn't make you connected. Having people not understand you makes you loneliest of all.

'Thank you.' I smile at Miss Jerris. Mr Newman has his back turned and doesn't see. Miss Jerris smiles back at me.

CHAPTER FIFTEEN

I'm late into the playground, where Grandad and Tim and Echo are waiting by Oscar and his mum.

Oscar is running around and around, and Echo is trying to join in but is fighting against his lead.

I grab Oscar's hand and say, 'What are you buzzing like a bee for?'

'We're all going swimming!' he shouts very loudly,

and I put my hands over my ears, screwing up my face.

'Sorry, Annie.' He stops running and says it again, much more quietly. I smile to let him know I'm grateful he understands.

'First summer swim of the year,' Grandad says. 'Oscar's mum said they were going to the beach too, so I thought we'd go together.'

'Hmm.'

I know I should give a more enthusiastic response, but I don't know about going to the beach with anyone else apart from my family. I'm not sure if the beach will change when I am on it with Oscar, or if it will still feel like my safe space. I like Oscar a lot, but I've never been with him outside of school and I'm not quite sure how it will be.

I'm quiet on our walk, but Oscar chatters away

to Tim, who is introducing him to Rabbit. Echo sticks close by my side, keeping me company in my nervousness.

'Echo, Echo, Echo, Echo,' I sing his name to him. I like the way the word repeats; I like that I am making an echo out of his name.

Echo wuffs. Tim and Oscar laugh, and then we all sing Echo's name together and run onto the sand.

We make a base camp for Grandad and Oscar's mum to watch us from, and take off our socks and shoes and change into wetsuits. I don't know what to do. I want to go and look for my tiny white shells, but Oscar wants me to swim.

Okay, I will swim with Oscar and then I will look for the shells. Grandad comes down to the edge of the water to keep an eye on us.

We run in and out of the sea, trying to get used

to the cold, cold water. I finally give up and belly-flop into the waves. Oscar copies me and takes in a mouthful of salty sea. He rises coughing and I pat his back again. It reminds me of lunchtime and I think again of the shells, but I'm okay here at the moment.

'Try this,' I tell him.

I get Oscar to lie on his back and I hold his shoulders as he stretches his arms and legs out into a star. 'I'm a floating starfish!' he giggles.

'Look up,' I say, and as I hold him and paddle my legs we look up at the big blue sky and the big white clouds high, high above. He's quiet and all I can hear is the sea waves lapping on the shore and the far-off birds circling and calling.

There is so much space around me, and when I look down I see I'm sharing it with Oscar, and yet it doesn't feel like I'm sharing it at all. Perhaps we can both be here together and it can mean even more.

When we're too cold and our fingers are going wrinkly and purple, we go onto the beach to dry off and play chase with Tim. Echo joins in and trips us all up as he leaps around.

Then I take Oscar to hunt for shells. He finds a big broken razor clam, two pebbles shaped like seals, a shiny piece of green sea glass and a dead crab. I find three whelks, an anemone that's orange-brown, and finally two tiny cream shells, just as I imagined.

I carry the shells up to where Grandad and Oscar's mum are sitting with the towels. I go to put them in my bag, and then I hesitate.

'Here.' I hand one to Oscar.

He holds it very carefully. 'Put it to your ear and

you'll hear the sea.' Solemnly, he does it and smiles as he listens. He goes to give it back.

'No, keep it. Listen to the sea tonight when you go to bed.'

Keeping only one shell isn't quite right for my colours today, but it is quite right for me and Oscar. And that feels a better thing.

CHAPTER SIXTEEN

It is a morning in late summer when Mum comes into my room and says, 'Annie, some of the pebbles and shells and sand need to go.'

I have one hundred and twenty-three items stacked up along my floor, my windowsill, my dressing table, even squished under the bed.

Some of them are jars of sand from when my days

are muddly. Others are smooth pebbles in grey, with pink flecks or jagged with sparkly white crystals. There are shiny clam shells, dried earthy seaweed, and ruffled, mottled feathers from gulls and razorbills and even an oyster catcher. Every day I have found at least one colour. Some days I've found a rainbow.

'No. No, no, no.' I hold on to yesterday's tiny black pebble.

'Yes. There's no space in your room. And you don't need them all.'

I do, I think. My knuckles clench around the stone. My fingers are all tight.

I look around my room. I see a rosy shell that matches my knuckles. I breathe and my hands loosen, darkening to their usual colour.

'I'm scared,' I say quietly.

Mum waits. If she asks more questions I start

confusing my feelings and thoughts and this makes them all blurry, and I get cross. I am glad she has remembered.

'I'm scared that I will forget how to do it. My colour treasures remind me that I can.'

'I can understand that. But what are you going to do when your room is filled up?'

'Fill up the rest of the house.'

There's a pause and then we both laugh. I imagine our home full to the brim with bits of the beach. It wouldn't be a home anymore.

'Let me think about it. I promise I will.'

'Alright. But if you don't come up with an idea by the weekend, I'll be removing them myself.'

Mum has understood, but not completely. I know I can't turn our house into the beach, but I don't know that I can find an answer by the weekend.

Mum's words have started an immediate countdown in my brain. There's a constant tick, tick, tick that I can't block out, reminding me every second that the deadline is getting closer. How can I find an answer when I don't know what it looks like? What will happen if I can't?

I snap at Tim and Grandad and Mum and am generally crotchety all day, even though I don't mean to be. I feel scared and trapped by the time.

We go to the beach after school like usual. I find two items today. A crab leg for being orange mad at Harry for pushing me at break time, and a shard of rock for being slow-worm grey at dinner when I realised I forgot to pack a spoon for my yoghurt. There's no colour for the ticking clock inside my head.

It's Tim who helps me find the solution. He has

been learning the days of the week at nursery and is chanting them over and over again while he digs a hole to 'Australia-land'.

'How many days in the week, Tim?' Grandad calls.

'Sixteen…three…twenty-two…'

Tim might have learnt the names, but he's not very good at numbers yet.

'It's seven, you noodle,' I say to him.

'Noooooooooodle,' he sings, waving a long, stringy bit of seaweed at me, and I tickle him until we're both collapsed and exhausted. The hurt of laughing a lot is a good hurt, like a tight hug under my ribs.

I sit back as he keeps on digging and I think.

If I start a week on Monday, I can collect seven days of colour. Then every Sunday I can come back to the beach and let them all go. It's like giving the beach back to itself. Rather than thinking I'm letting go of what I can do, I can see it as releasing that week's stress. It can settle back into part of something bigger again. I don't know how it will feel to let things go. I don't know if it will be possible. But it's an idea, and it's my own. My tummy feels warm for having thought out a solution by myself.

Mum gives me a big hug when I explain it to her. 'All you can do is try,' she says, reminding me that trying is all I can ever do. About the colours, about managing myself.

So I do.

The next day, Grandad gets out his wheelbarrow, and I spend the morning bringing my stones and shells and seaweed and glass and feathers and driftwood downstairs and putting them in the wheelbarrow. By the time I'm only left with yesterday's stone and crab leg, there's a big heap.

All five of us wheel it down to the beach. We push the wheelbarrow across the sand right to the cliff end. It takes ages but we keep pushing, even Tim. I look back and see the wiggly line of the wheel, the four sets of footprints alongside the paw tracks from Echo.

Echo comes beside me and I bend down. 'I can do this, can't I?' He licks my nose. I lean and smell his coat. He's warm and soft and safe. Then I stand up and Echo sits by my heels.

Mum, Grandad, Tim and I push the barrow up on its end and the contents clatter-crash out in a river of colours.

'It's the biggest pile of treasures ever!' Tim wants to dig into it, but Mum stops him.

It's above the tide now, but I know it won't stay there forever. As the sea comes up, the treasures will break down onto the beach, get pulled out by the waves. They will scatter through the water, spreading out and away.

I place my hand on Echo's head and feel his warm fur. Maybe the treasures will get washed back, and maybe they'll land on another beach for someone else to find. I breathe in and out and follow my shells and stones and feathers in my mind, as we all are, drifting free.

Made in United States
North Haven, CT
09 October 2021

10249342R00069